S0-DUS-886

WE ARE ALL GUILTY

Kingsley Amis

WE ARE ALL GUILTY

IN ASSOCIATION WITH
REINHARDT BOOKS

VIKING/REINHARDT BOOKS

Published by the Penguin Group
Penguin Books Ltd, 27 Wrights Lane, London W8 5TZ, England
Penguin Books USA Inc., 375 Hudson Street, New York, New York 10014, USA
Penguin Books Australia Ltd, Ringwood, Victoria, Australia
Penguin Books Canada Ltd, 10 Alcorn Avenue, Toronto, Ontario, Canada M4V 3B2
Penguin Books (NZ) Ltd, 182–190 Wairau Road, Auckland 10, New Zealand

Penguin Books Ltd, Registered Offices: Harmondsworth, Middlesex, England

First published 1991
Published by Viking 1991
1 3 5 7 9 10 8 6 4 2

Printed in England by Clays Ltd, St Ives plc
Filmset in Sabon

A CIP catalogue record for this book is available from the British Library
ISBN 0–670–84268–0

TO

JUDY

FOREWORD

During my writing life I suppose I must have made up several hundred characters of various shapes and sizes, jobs and age-groups. I cannot help rather liking all of them, even the most unpleasant, because in their different ways they are all parts of me. But usually, when I finish a story or a novel I am quite glad to have finished with the people in it, however fond I might have been of some of them, and feel impatient to get on with the next lot.

A couple of times, though, I have felt I had to bring somebody back. One was a working-class girl from the North, Jenny Bunn. I wrote a novel about her at the start of the Sixties, but she would not let me alone and I had to write about her again in 1988. Clive Rayner, a seventeen-year-old out-of-work Cockney lad, stayed around too. I thought I had done with him in a Seventies TV play, but last year I realized I was still thinking of him and his life. This short book is the result.

Clive is utterly unlike me. I have never had any of his experiences and I have never known anyone who has. But I found as I wrote that I cared more about him than about any of my previous male characters that I could remember. Of course I read the papers, and I have eyes and ears. I must have made the rest up.

Kingsley Amis

I

Clive Rayner lived with his mother and stepfather in a small terrace house near one of the approach-roads to the western flyover. The end house had been turned into a cigarette and newspaper place, empty now like the house next but two to it. The road used to lead somewhere, but it had been blocked off by a hoarding before the family moved in and was now a cul-de-sac. Between the back of the terrace and a derelict furniture-factory, there lay a stretch of tussocky grass littered with out-of-date refrigerators and other unwanted household gear. Behind the empty house stood a half-demolished cage of wood slats and chicken-wire. No one knew what it had once contained.

There were no buildings opposite, and the terrace looked out only on to the flyover and the road leading up to it. But the inside of no. 9, where Clive lived, was well cared for, neat and comfortable. His mother worked hard on it and was a good second-hand shopper, and his stepfather, a jobbing carpenter, was useful too. With the help of the glass screens he had made and put up inside the front windows, the traffic noise was reduced to a level where the family hardly noticed it, except occasionally at night.

Although he would rather not have had to spend so much of his time there, Clive had no great objection to being at home, at any rate when his stepfather was out at work or round the pub. He was called Don MacIntyre, so his father or whoever it was must have come from Scotland, though he talked with an accent from somewhere up the north of England. Perhaps one place or the other came into his religious thing. God and Christ and all that side of it hardly got mentioned, except when he was ticking Clive off for using bad language, but he went on a lot about stuff like a sense of duty, responsibility and honesty like an old-fashioned vicar, and was always at Clive for not having them or not living up to them. Compared to some stepfathers he had heard about, Clive would have had to admit that maybe Don was not too bad, but he was pretty fair hell to get on with.

One afternoon when he was alone in the house and there was nothing on TV, Clive felt he must get out of the place, even just for an hour or so. He rang up his mate Terry and arranged to meet him in the usual spot. They called it that because they thought it sounded better than the coffee-shop along the Parade. To get to it without going a long way round, Clive climbed up a steep bank of dirty grass and weeds and walked along the side of the approach-road. There was a sort of walkway there, just wide enough for one careful person, and probably only meant for emergencies. Sometimes a passing driver would hoot or yell at him and Clive would swear back. Then after about sixty yards there was a gap where an alley-way led round to the Parade.

On the outward journey along the walkway Clive had the cars facing him and collected a hoot and a yell or two. Coming home there was nothing, or nothing until he was stepping off it on to the grassy bank above the terrace. Then a car that had been coming up from behind pulled in and drew up just there. Clive had hardly had time to see it was a police car before a man's voice spoke over the lowered passenger window.

'Hey, you there, having trouble?' The tone was sharp but not aggressive.

Clive knew of nothing that should have made him afraid of the police, though of course he resented them, like all his mates. 'No,' he said without any expression.

'In that case, what were you doing walking along there?' Still no aggression. 'You're not supposed to, there, unless you have to.'

'I was just taking a short cut.'

'Wait a minute. Stay where you are.'

A tall man in his forties got out of the car. Although he would have had to be some sort of policeman he was wearing an ordinary office suit, dark and conservative, with a tie that looked well chosen to go with his light-blue shirt. Apart from a good deal of hair gone, he was quite handsome in a way for his age. He seemed on the alert, looking Clive over as he strolled up to him, but not full of himself or unfriendly like some of them.

'Now, did I hear you say something about a short cut?' he asked.

When Clive explained a bit, the policeman went on looking him over, not listening much. For a moment Clive thought he might be a poofter, then turned down that idea – the guy's stare was too cold.

'Inspector, are you?'

'Sergeant. What's your name, sonny?'

'Have I got to tell you?'

'Certainly not, don't if you don't feel like it. Just asking.'

If Clive had been less completely in the dark, he might not have given his name like a good boy. 'Why, you looking for somebody?' he wanted to know.

'No. Not specially.' The fellow had a rather officer-class accent for a copper. 'And you're what, Clive, eighteen?'

'Seventeen.'

The sergeant looked at his watch. 'I suppose you wouldn't have anything in the way of a job?'

'Not regular.'

'What, a great big healthy fellow like you not got a proper job? Bags of jobs going in these parts. London Transport's crying out for young blokes. Not worth your while for the extra few nicker, I dare say. Still, I don't imagine you want to discuss that, do you? No, well, er . . . Actually, I was looking for somebody, to be quite honest.' But he left out saying the somebody was not Clive. After a moment, he went on, 'Might as well run you home, I suppose, after keeping you talking like this.'

'Not worth it, I live just down there.' Clive pointed.

'Oh, *there*. In the terrace. I see.'

'Is that important?'

'No, no. Not important. How long have you been living there?'

'Couple of years. Why?'

'With your parents?'

'My mother and stepfather.'

'I see.' The sergeant sounded as though he saw a lot. He nodded his head and half turned for another glance towards the house. 'I'll be getting along, then,' he said, finally. 'See you again, Clive.'

He went back to the car and was driven away. His manner had stayed cool, well on the right side of bullying or rude, but as Clive half ran, half skidded down the slope he was a bit worried. What had that guy been after? Being a copper he was sure to have been up to no good, but what sort of no good? And 'see you again' – was that supposed to be some sort of threat? Then Clive told himself things were coming to a pretty pass if he was going to let a nosy bloody pig get him down, and by the time he let himself into no. 9 he had forgotten all about it.

That was easy anyway, because as soon as he got into the kitchen, where they mostly sat, he knew there was something going on. He had expected his mother to be there; she was usually back from her cleaning by now, but Don was home early, meaning he would have missed an hour or more's pay, which would have done nothing to sweeten his temper. There was more to it than that, though.

'Ah, here comes the young lord and master,' he said in his flat northern brogue, 'back from working his fingers to the bone to swell the family exchequer. Sit down, lad.'

Clive sat, but did his best to look as if he had been going to anyway. 'Got a cup of tea there, Mum?'

'I'll make you some fresh,' said his mother, who seemed to be trying to flash him a kind of warning.

Don took a couple of paces up and down the room, like some smartypants bloody lawyer, Clive thought to himself. 'You've come in at just the right time, lad,' said his stepfather. 'For the moment you just listen. Right, as your mother and I were saying. Alice, have I ever been through your handbag before to your knowledge? At any time?'

Immediately Clive knew what his mother's warning had been about, and sat still in his chair for a moment with his eyes down, before he remembered to relax and look bored.

'No, never, Don,' his mother was saying. 'See, I just thought you could have found yourself a bit short, you know, and gone and –'

'Will you listen to me, Alice? I said to you just a moment ago, if I'd taken it, not that I ever would have done but *if* I had, I'd have told you straight away, no hanging about. Come on, wouldn't I?'

'Yes, Don. I was only just wondering . . .' Her voice trailed away.

'Wondering? If I'd done it and forgotten? Something like that?'

'No, of course not. Just . . . you know.'

Don stood up straight, like a lawyer who has got something important out of a witness or someone. (So far, Clive had never actually been in a law court, but he watched a lot of TV.) 'Ay, I know, I know indeed,' said Don in a satisfied voice, 'I should do by now. You're just trying to think of something to help out that . . . miserable son of yours. He took it. Of course he took it. You realize that yourself, don't you?'

'If I did,' said Clive's mother, 'do you think I'd have let you know about it? Make you a present of it, like, for you to go on at him about?'

She was quite fly in that sort of way, Clive had noticed before, looking harmless and a bit helpless but able to come out with things like that. It threw Don for a moment, but he was soon off again.

'Well,' he said, 'you were . . . you weren't thinking, ay, you brought it up before you realized the, er, the implications of what you were saying. Mind, I'm right glad you did! A thief in the house! Not that I'm surprised, I'll have you know. Just a question of time.'

'Oh, Don, please,' said Clive's mother, sounding quite helpless now.

'No, Alice, please let me, let me say what I have to

say.' He came and stood in front of Clive, showing off his hook nose and eyes that bulged a bit. 'You're playing a very dangerous game, lad. I hope you're wise to that. Like all your precious generation. Like the whole bloody country, top to bottom. No respect, no respect for anything at all. If you see something you fancy or something you think you need, grab it, that's the motto, never mind who it belongs to, who paid for it. But you can't go on for ever, you know. There's always a day of reckoning. Be sure your sin will find you out.'

Clive's mother looked up from making tea, but Clive spoke before she could.

'No, Mum,' he said.

She added, 'If you own up now, then we can . . .'

'I said no. I didn't.'

'Who was it, then?' asked Don. 'The old girl next door nipped in? Window-cleaner? Batman?'

'Look, I only said it wasn't me.'

An expression of awful enjoyment came over Don's face. 'Are you willing to swear to that?'

'Yeah, I don't mind,' said Clive.

'On this?' Hardly having to look round, Don reached behind him to the kitchen cupboard, which had a row of books along it behind the vinegar and the pickle-jars, and brought out the old leather-covered Bible he was sometimes seen looking things up in.

'All right with me,' said Clive, and he was just going to put his hand on it, as he had seen people do in films, when Don's face changed and he snatched it away.

'No!' he almost shouted. 'I'm not going to let you. It'd be . . .' Sometimes he looked really mad, off his head. Then he said, more calmly, 'Your whole trouble comes from your lack of religion.'

Clive considered he had taken about enough. His turn now. And his mother was pouring tea, not looking at them, not on his side at all, but not on Don's either. Right, then.

'So you said before once or twice,' he told his stepfather. 'Didn't do you much good, did it, religion? Three months for assault? That's worse than anything I ever done.'

'All right, lad, I done wrong and I paid for it.'

'Good for you,' said Clive with a sneer. 'Must be a great feeling, though.' He did a pretend punch at the air and put on a hick accent. 'Boof! Take that in the name of the Lord, you bastard!'

That was almost too much for Don. Clive's mother quickly held out a mug of tea in front of him and that seemed to bring him round.

'Pack it up, you two!' she said sharply. 'All this carry-on over a lousy tenner!'

One of Don's troubles was, he was so bloody predictable. 'Lousy tenner!' he said, nearly shouting again. 'What's it matter how much? Tenner or ten thousand or ten p makes not a blind bit of difference. It's the principle of the thing.'

'Ah, yeah,' said Clive, but he said it quietly, almost to himself.

'Any case,' said his mother, 'I'm not that sure it's gone.'

'What?' said Don. 'But you –'

'Not hundred per cent.'

Don shook his head slowly. 'You couldn't have . . .'

'I remember thinking at the supermarket, it come to more than I expected. Everything's gone up, everyone says. I *could* have changed it, that note.'

'Did you keep that slip with the purple figures they give you with the prices all added up? Sort of strip of stiff paper?'

'I suppose I might have, yeah.'

'You're not sure.'

'No. Can't think where I put it if I did. Sorry.'

'All right.' Don turned his back on the two of them and went to the side of the sink and looked out of the window, where there was never anything worth looking at. Clive heard him sigh. After a minute he turned round, said 'All right' again and went to the door. 'I'm going up now to have a wash and brush-up and then I'll be going out for an hour or so, okay? And nobody need think anyone's got away with anything. Understood? Just remember that.'

He made a great business of shutting the door quietly behind him. Him going off was a relief for Clive, until he noticed the expression on his mother's face.

'Sorry, Mum.'

'Your tea all right? Come and sit down here at the table where I can see you. Now Clive, I don't like having to lie, whether it's to help you or anybody else. Well, it wasn't quite lying, because I wasn't quite sure, not to swear to it, and of course I hoped I was wrong.

So I had to do the best I could for you, that was only fair. Now, I say I wasn't sure, but I knew all right, and if I hadn't done straight away, I would have before you'd been in the room here two minutes. I knew as certain as if I'd seen you take that note out of my bag with my own eyes. No, don't deny it, don't you dare try and lie to me again, don't say anything, just listen to me. You won't get another chance. You understand me? You do anything like that again, and I won't lift a finger to protect you, it's no good. If he wants to, if Don wants to get the police in I won't even try to stop him. Have you got that, Clive?'

Clive had got it all right and he was badly shaken. He had never seen his mother angry like this before. There was another feeling, worse in a way because it made no sense at all, that somehow that plain-clothes sergeant had known or guessed about that tenner, no, that was impossible, but seen he was a thief. Recognized his type. Still confused, not thinking much, Clive asked, 'Say all that in front of him, would you, Mum? Just like that?'

'No, Clive, I don't suppose I would.'

'Neat him skipping out like that, then, wasn't it? Handy, like.'

They heard water from upstairs running away. Clive's mother said, 'Handy? He went out when he did so I could talk to you alone. Didn't you see him give me the nod? No, of course you didn't. Your trouble is, you're dead stupid, Clive. Thick. You don't notice what's going on round you. You're not even interested.

You go everywhere with your eyes shut. No wonder you're bored out of your mind.'

Still talking, she went over to the stove. 'I know Don's just a bloody Christer to you and a pest with a silly accent, but you just start trying to realize that him and me are husband and wife, and that means we understand each other pretty well without having to say a lot. About you, for instance.'

'So the pair of you can gang up on me,' said Clive, feeling awful now.

'No, so we can get you to see sense, or try. For your own good. Yeah, I know you're thinking that that's what *he* says, but it's true. Clive.' She went on more quietly, 'Get this bit too. You're my son. Always. Whatever you do. You must know that.' She gave him a little smile, but he thought he saw a tear in her eye. 'It means I'll always do my best for you, and it's up to you to try to always do your best for me. But that doesn't mean to say we have a nice hug and a fag and forget all about it now, and I give you another tenner just to show there's no ill-feeling. I think tonight would be a very good night for you to go out with your mates. But before you go you can pop along to the Lord Harry and fetch me back a couple of bottles of Guinness. Oh . . .' – she squeezed his hand for a moment – 'sorry I called you stupid, dear, but, well, you don't *think* much, do you?'

2

By ten to seven, when Clive got back to the Lord Harry after delivering his mother's Guinness, the music was going pretty loud, not as loud as it would be when the group got going about eight, but loud enough for him not to have to say much to Terry. That suited him fine. Clive was in a mood, meaning not just he was pissed off, though he was pissed off, meaning more he was still a bit shaken up by what his mother had said to him about himself. It bothered him she should think he was stupid, even though she had half taken it back after she calmed down. What was he supposed to do, start to be a scientist, fly a bloody plane, be on the Council, do things on television? How? With what? That was meant to happen at school, starting anything like that, and at Clive's school, which he remembered almost nothing about bar sitting wanting to go home, it had been no good expecting to start anything at all, not even being a teacher.

He had got this far, frowning over his lager, when

he saw past Terry's shoulder Marilyn and Paula coming from the street into the patchy light and darkness of the pub. Terry gave them a wave, and they must have seen, because they came over and sat down, but neither of them looked at him or Clive or smiled. There seemed to be a sort of agreement between them that they would turn up and go along, but saw no reason to put themselves out to be pleasant or sociable. They talked to each other a bit, if one of them frowning and moving her lips and the other one shrugging her shoulders and sniffing, that type of stuff, counted as talking to each other. When they took a drink off Clive it was like they were doing him a favour.

By the time they went outside it was dark, but most of the shops had lights on and there were buses and stuff. Marilyn and Paula went in front, because the other way round Clive and Terry kept having to go back for them when they stopped and looked into shop windows. Clive never did that except when anybody would, like passing a TV shop. He was not going to be buying anything.

Terry started telling him about a couple of blokes he knew at work. For a minute Clive just let him carry on, but then he remembered what his mother had said to him about not noticing what was going on round him, and so he started listening, but Terry had a job. What he was saying never stuck to anything or got anywhere. It was like when a kid was trying to explain about a movie he had seen. Pathetic really, thought Clive, but told himself to forget that, because Terry was a good old lad, cheerful and never asking questions and someone to be with.

The four of them had stopped outside the Bengal Light and were just starting to shuffle towards the door when something made Clive look over his shoulder and across the road. A police car was halted there. It could have been the one that that sergeant had been riding in, but there were dozens of others like it. At the wheel, there was a uniformed man looking in their direction, and on the far side of him somebody else, whom Clive could not see properly. After a second or two the driver turned his head away and the car began to move off.

Terry had tried to pick up what Clive had noticed and not managed it, but he saw Clive's face. 'What's up, mate?' he asked.

'Eh? Nothing, why?' said Clive, and turned away towards the restaurant. 'Why?'

'I don't know, I just thought you saw something. I don't know. You hungry, Clive?'

Clive was trying to make up his mind that of course that had been just any old police car, just happened to be there, had to be somewhere. And they had nothing on him.

'Well, I'm bloody starving,' said Terry. 'I'm going to have a whole tandoori chicken.'

Being where it was, the place was not trying to make itself smart. It had thick furry dark-red wallpaper crap and tables along the walls with old-fashioned spindly gilt domes over each one, with music to match. As usual, there was plenty of room. One of the fellows there sat them down, all flashing eyes and very fussy and polite-spoken, but underneath obviously thinking they were dirt.

Still, they all cheered up at the idea of getting fed. The two birds got quite perky, chattering away to each other but starting to notice Clive and Terry. They ordered lagers and Bombay duck, and Terry made his usual supposed-to-be-joke about Bombay duck, and Paula and Marilyn made their usual shocked noises, and then no one said anything for a bit, which was noticeable now there was no music. Well, there was the usual Paki wailing and jangling, but nothing like the rock in the Lord Harry, and when they had given their order things started to go flat again, so Clive thought he might as well tell them about the row over the tenner.

Terry sounded rather as though he was talking for the sake of talking himself when he said, 'Oh yeah, well, kind of dull of you, Clive, wasn't it, going and taking it like that? I mean, you know, bound to, er . . .'

'Eh? Bound to what?' Clive asked, already bored with it all.

'Well, I thought your mum was supposed to be on your side and everything. This isn't going to help that, is it?'

Paula chipped in. She was the one who was meant to be Clive's girl-friend, which he sometimes thought boiled down to him being the one she went for when she wanted to work off a peeve, which was quite often.

‘All this fuss about nicking,’ she said. ‘Why couldn’t you just go and *ask* her? She must know you’ve only got your Giro money coming in regular.’

‘She wouldn’t have given it to me,’ said Clive. ‘I told you. She’s scared stiff of *him*, see? More than her life’s worth to go against him.’

‘What’s the matter with him, then?’

‘Nothing a kick in the head wouldn’t put right,’ said Clive. He said it viciously to impress Paula and because he knew he had lied about his mother being scared of Don.

‘No, I mean, you know, wrong with him,’ said Paula, not impressed.

‘Bloody Scotch, isn’t he?’

‘Eh?’ said Marilyn. She was dumber than Paula but seemed not to go in for peeves, not so much.

‘He’s one of the bloody Scotch,’ explained Clive in a patient voice. ‘My stepfather is a bloody Scotchman from Scotland. All right?’

‘I thought you were telling us he was north-country,’ said Paula, glaring at Clive.

‘He is, but he comes from Scotland, he came from Scotland, his mum and dad came from Scotland, got it?’

‘What?’ asked Marilyn.

‘You can tell by the Mac.’

Terry and the girls all stared blankly at Clive, who said furiously, ‘The Mac in his name! I told you, he’s called Mac – Intyre. Christ Almighty!’

After another silence, Terry said, ‘Anyway, what’s

that got to do with it? Your stepfather being from Scotland.'

'Well, don't blame it on me, but up there they go in for preaching and sin and the Bible and that,' said Clive, calming down. 'He wanted me to swear on the Bible I hadn't ripped off that bloody tenner.'

'Well, did you?' asked Terry.

'No, he changed his mind.'

'Suppose he hadn't, would you have sworn on the Bible?'

'What are you, Tel, a bloody copper? Of course I'd have sworn on the Bible. Why not? What could happen? A flash of lightning sent down by the Lord?'

That made Terry wriggle a bit, as Clive had known it would. Neither of the birds had any idea what he was talking about. Then the waiter started bringing the food, so there was no need to say anything more, and they all went on not saying anything while they ate.

Clive tried to work his way through a lamb curry that was rather hotter than he really liked – to ask for a mild one was not on. He remembered what his mother had said about him going round with his eyes shut, and to pass the time now he tried to imagine what she would think of the other three, sort of see them through her eyes. What with one thing and another he was still upset, but that seemed to help rather than not.

He saw Paula with her hair in stiff spikes, wearing a mucky black T-shirt and black mini-skirt, thick purple woollen stockings and chunky boots with rainbow laces, Marilyn with a very short haircut like a bloke's, in black studded leather all over and again bloke's boots, Terry with swept-back wet-look hair . . . Christ, thought Clive, why have I never seen it till now? Not shocking or ugly or even a joke. Bloody *silly*. Ridiculous. Pathetic. There was another word. Contemptible. And where did that leave him, with his pony-tail, maroon jacket and shiny skin-tight pants?

Just then, Marilyn took a bone out of her mouth and, with a smear of chutney on her lip, said, 'Isn't Mac Irish?'

'Eh? How do you mean?' said Terry.

'You know – Mac. Name, sort of bit of a name. Irish, ennit.'

'That's O you're thinking of, brainy,' said Paula. 'Like O'Riley.'

'O'Neil,' said Terry. 'Yeah.'

'There's this girl at work,' said Marilyn, 'goes out with a bloke called MacManus, and he's Irish.'

'Can't be,' said Terry. 'Well, I don't know, he could be, couldn't he?'

'He bloody *is*. You ought to hear him, you know, his brogue. Comes from Dublin. That's Ireland.'

'That's right,' said Terry.

Paula was going to say something, but Clive broke in. He thought he would go mad if any of them said another word. 'Shut up, the lot of you,' he told them, not loudly, but they all kept quiet and sat still. He took out the tenner he had stolen from his mother and put it on the table with some coins. 'Terry. Get the bill and pay. And quick about it. I'll be outside. Quick about it, mind.'

It was a good thing that nobody, like a waiter carrying dishes, got in Clive's way as he made for the door, because for two pins he would have seen them off without thinking twice. In the street a bit of a cold wind had sprung up and he shivered. He thought that the people who hurried past him were keeping well away from him. Just as well for them. The traffic all seemed quite normal. Clive wished Terry would get things moving and not give him time to come down from the sort of high he had quite suddenly found himself on.

Here they were at last. With Terry trailing behind, he hustled Paula and Marilyn to their bus-stop, taking no notice of what they said about wanting a coffee or about anything else. When the bus came they tried not to get on it, but Clive said, shouting a bit, that they could suit themselves, he and Terry were off, and he just walked away and left them.

Clive and Terry went for a coffee and sat for a couple of minutes without saying anything.

'What was that about you and me being off?' asked Terry. 'Anywhere in particular?'

'I'm thinking, all right?'

'What's the matter with you? You've been funny all evening. You're sweating.'

'I'm hot,' said Clive. If he had been used to putting his feelings into words he might have gone on to say that for a moment back there he had seen what his life was like, seen what it was, just nothing, and knew he would never have a life like other people, and knew he was completely alone. But even if he had been able to work it out like that, instead of dimly but powerfully feeling it, he could never have started to tell Terry. So what he said was, 'You know Butterfield Brothers?'

'Yeah. Warehouse place, ennit. Just round the corner from here.'

'You and me, we're going to do it.'

'What? Why, what's there? What are you talking about?'

'Electrical . . . apparatus,' said Clive. 'And that kind of thing.'

'How do you mean?'

'Toasters are electrical. And fires. I don't know. Lots of stuff. We'll see what there is when we get in there.'

'What, you mean break in and pinch stuff?'

'Got it, mastermind. Let's get going, we're wasting time.'

'But there'll be dogs and guards,' said Terry, still blinking in surprise and shock, but getting on his feet. 'You know, Securicor. You know, blokes with helmets and sticks.'

'Not there, it's all run down. And they always have a notice saying about dogs and guards if there's any there, or even if there isn't, and they don't have one there. We can get over that gate in half a minute flat.'

Clive turned out to be right about the gate of Butterfield Bros., and he and Terry soon had a window broken, in fact it was cracked already so it was more just pushing it in, and soon they were inside the place with no trouble at all. They looked round. There was not much to see, apart from damp-stains, empty metal containers and a steep narrow staircase leading to a narrow catwalk with a guard-rail along it. Clive led the way up the stairs and they had just reached the catwalk when a bell started ringing some distance off.

Terry pulled at the back of Clive's bomber jacket. 'Come on, let's get out of here,' he said in a loud whisper.

'Shut up and listen. I don't think there's anyone around.'

The bell stopped and silence followed. Half a minute. More.

'Right, move it,' said Clive. 'Just automatic, that thing.'

He turned a corner, still on the catwalk, and straight away a man came out of an opening in the wall and started running towards him and shouting, a stocky middle-aged man with a clipped moustache. He looked and sounded quite fierce and this catwalk thing, ten or fifteen feet from the floor, was no place to start an argument. In no time at all Clive and Terry were running back the way they had come as fast as they could, which was not very fast with so little room to spare.

Terry got to the top of the staircase, then Clive, who had noticed that just there the guard-rail had broken away and been roughly repaired with wood and wire. And it was just there that the man chasing them caught the collar of Clive's jacket. They struggled for a moment, Clive only trying to get free, not hitting the man or even pushing him, but unintentionally throwing him off balance. The man's foot slipped on the metal and he grabbed at the weak part of the rail. It gave way and he cried out and fell, landing below with a thump that Clive never forgot.

But for now he thought only of getting away. He clattered down the stairs at top speed, saw an outside door, ran to it and started shifting bolts. He shouted to Terry to come on, and Terry shouted back something about the bloke being hurt. Clive wasted no more time, but got the door open and ran out.

3

'Hallo, Clive, fancy seeing you. I know I said we'd run into each other again, but frankly I didn't expect it to be so soon after our first meeting.' The plain-clothes sergeant looked at his watch and raised his eyebrows. 'Yes, less than five hours. Actually I was on the point of going off duty when they brought you in.' He smiled. 'You just caught me in time.'

Clive and Terry were sitting in a police interview room, having been picked up by a patrol car pretty well as they were leaving Butterfield Bros. and fetched to this station. It was a small, rather stuffy room without windows, but painted in light colours. Also there was a uniformed police constable who had taken statements from the two. These the sergeant was now glancing through, having just come in and given Clive what would have been a horrible shock if he had not felt so exhausted, like if he had run a mile, he thought, though he had no way of knowing.

'Yes, I see . . . of course . . .' the plain-clothes man

muttered as he read, then looked up to say, 'Oh – my name's Parnell, Sergeant Parnell, and this is Constable Evans.'

'How do you do,' said Terry quite seriously, like an idiot. He was obviously cheered up by the meek-and-mild way this Sergeant Parnell guy was going on, but Clive knew better and kept his eyes and ears skinned.

'Yes, that seems quite clear,' said the sergeant. 'Ah, here we are, Clive – "the watchman caught me by my collar and I pulled away and he yelled out and fell off the staircase." Is that really all that happened, Clive? You must have punched him or something, surely, to make him fall like that.'

'Think about it before you answer,' said the constable in a rough, tough sort of voice. He had a red face and hairy eyebrows.

'All right, all right, Jack,' said the sergeant. 'Clive's thinking about it, aren't you, Clive?'

'Well, of course I am.' Clive was laughing his head off without letting it show. So here it was for real – the old hard cop and soft cop set-up everybody had heard about. 'Er . . . no, like I said, I just pulled away. It was very slippery along there, you can check.'

Sergeant Parnell nodded seriously. 'Yes, we'll be looking into that. Important point, Jack. Now, you two, I'll get you to sign these in a moment, but first I'd like to ask you a few questions in an informal sort of way. We find it helps if we get as complete a picture of a case as we reasonably can – I'm sure you understand that.'

'Oh, yeah,' said Terry in his good-boy style.

'Fine,' said the sergeant. He sounded relieved. 'Now, have either of you two lads ever been in any kind of trouble before?'

Clive thought he might as well go along for the time being. 'I got pulled in one Saturday last year down Furnace Park. It turned a bit hairy in the second half, and I, er, well, the police started to move in . . .'

'Just tell me what happened in your own words.'

'I was with this mate of mine, see,' said Clive, all honest and straightforward, 'and this copper starts lugging him off, and I went to give him a hand, you know, and another copper grabs me, and there's a set-to, like.'

'Did you hit him, or kick him, or anything?'

'Not really,' said Clive. 'More a struggle was all.'

'I see. Were you arrested, Clive?'

'I don't know what you call arrested. There was about a dozen of us and they took our names and the end of it was they let us go.'

Sergeant Parnell nodded his head without speaking. Now he seemed a bit stumped.

'Aren't you going to write any of that down?' asked Clive.

'I'll remember what I need to remember, sonny. Thanks all the same. Now . . . Terry. What about you?'

'Nothing like that, sir,' said Terry as though he was shocked to be asked.

'Oh, well there we are. Next question. Is there

anything in your circumstances at home, either of you, that might make the court tend to go a bit easy on you? You know the kind of thing, mother a widow, bad housing conditions, father a drunk, violent, anything at all of that sort. Take your time.'

'Well . . .' Clive started to say.

'Yes? Go on. Feel free. Now's your chance.'

'Well, my mum and dad got a divorce seven years ago and my mum married a bloke called MacIntyre.'

'Yes, now we might be on to something. Tell me about Mr MacIntyre, Clive.'

Clive did, ending up by saying, 'He done three months in the slammer a while back for punching up a fellow in a pub. For using bad language, according to him.'

'Really.' The sergeant looked very interested. 'Now that *is* a point, eh Jack?' He made a note. 'Three . . . months. A problem family. What about you, Terry?'

'Nothing at all in that line, sir,' said Terry. 'I was trying to think. Very respectable, my folks. My dad works at the public library.'

'Oh, he does, does he? Pity, that. Still, I'm sure you won't actually suffer for it.' The sergeant took a good look at Terry and at Clive, smiling with his eyes half-closed. 'What made you do it, lads? There was nothing there worth your while, or didn't you know that?'

Clive said, 'A lark, really.'

'That's right,' said Terry. 'Of course, we can see it was wrong now.'

'Of course you can, son. Well, that's about all for the moment. You got anything, Jack?'

Clive had been bringing out his cigarette and lighter. He put a fag in his mouth and just glanced at the sergeant and the constable. They stared back at him with no expression on their faces at all. Clive lit up, keeping the packet in his hand. The sergeant started pacing the room.

'What'll happen to us, sir?' Terry asked.

'Oh, now let's see, who's on tomorrow? Yes . . . Er, the chances are you'll be remanded on bail for a week or so, brought up again and fined, put on probation . . .' Terry relaxed on hearing this, but not Clive. 'After all,' the sergeant went on, 'you were no trouble to catch, walked into our arms as you might say, and you didn't resist arrest, you hadn't taken anything. Of course, if it was left to me . . .' The sergeant paused here and nodded his head to the constable, who got up and started to come over. When the sergeant spoke again, the tone of his voice was just the same as before, light and conversational, interested. 'If it was left to me, the two of you would go down for five years apiece in an unreconstructed old-time prison with what used to be known as hard labour, which was very hard indeed. Actively unpleasant, in fact.'

Very quickly and neatly, as if he had been specially trained to the job, Sergeant Parnell snatched the cigarette out of Clive's mouth, knocked the packet from his hand and ground them both thoroughly into the floor. The constable stood by.

'Yes,' said the sergeant, 'five years without remission in an unheated building would be something for you to remember, to take into consideration, the next time you felt like a lark.'

'Mind you,' said the constable, 'it's no picnic even today, my young friends.'

'We can't be sent to prison,' said Clive as toughly as he could, 'we're under eighteen.'

'Shut up, you little brute,' said the sergeant, not speaking conversationally now, 'and both of you listen to me. Now – in the next couple of weeks you're going to meet a lot of people who feel sorry for you and don't want to punish you and would give anything to understand you. I'd just like you to know that there are one or two people around who don't feel sorry for you and do want to punish you and understand you already, top to bottom. You're scum, the pair of you, and you'll never hear about it, except from me. I'm going to do everything in my power to see that you get a bad time. I don't expect to succeed, because this whole place, the whole system, the whole country's rotten with so-called experts and social workers and psychiatrists and psychologists and what-not who've forgotten two little words – right and wrong. But you needn't think you're going to get away with it –'

He stopped because there was a knock at the door. 'Excuse me,' he said offensively and went and opened it. He had a very short conversation with a young policewoman, but it was long enough for her to notice

Clive giving her the once-over and to send him back a freezer that went all the way down to his stomach. The door shut.

'As I was saying,' the sergeant continued, soon getting back to the level of controlled violence he had been on before, 'it would be silly of you to run away with the idea that you'll go on getting off scot-free for ever. When you've done this kind of caper a few more times – which you will – and been caught a few more times – which you will be – you're even going to get those experts annoyed, you're going to show up their theories for the rubbish they are. And as soon as you're old enough, you'll start going to prison – oh, ping-pong, woodwork, colour TV and the rest of it, but it'll still be prison.'

'Up at four, lights out nine o'clock,' said the constable.

The sergeant had been talking entirely to Clive most of the time, and went on like that. 'Yes, I could write your life story before it happens. In fact I could have done that after one minute's confab by the flyover. You're an open book, Clive. Right, if you'll just sign these statements, the two of you, or put a cross on them . . .'

'I can write,' said Clive. It came out less tough this time.

The sergeant leapt at it. 'Can you now, sonny? Can you really? Peculiar sort of school you got yourself into, wasn't it? Taught you to write? Whatever happened to self-expression?'

Without looking at each other, the two lads set about signing where the constable pointed.

'Sorry, I suppose I shouldn't have said that last bit,' said the sergeant, shaking his head and frowning. 'Rather on the cheap side, I'm afraid. Been on duty too long. Oh, by the way, that message I got just now. From the hospital. The night watchman. They're keeping him in.'

'What's that mean?' asked Terry.

'What's it mean? Might mean anything from a couple of days' treatment for bruises to the big one,' said Sergeant Parnell. 'But what do you care, eh? You've had your lark.'

When he was completely fed up with sitting around in his cramped little bedroom, where a water-tank shook and made noises at all hours, and had had enough of staring at the photographs of pop stars he had stuck on the walls, Clive went downstairs and into the kitchen. He had heard his stepfather come in and knew he would have to face him sooner or later. When he talked to his mother and tried to explain and said he was sorry, she had not wanted to know, not really, so there was her too to face in a way.

'All right, lad, I'm not going to eat you,' said Don in what he probably thought was an easy-going, helpful sort of style. 'Believe me, it would be no trouble at all for me to fly off the handle, but I've promised not to.' He looked at Clive's mother, who was sitting closer up to him than she usually did. Clive got the message and sort of swallowed hard and settled himself opposite them.

'Now, first things first,' said Don. 'And in the present case first things is that watchman, as I hope you agree. Do you? Do you agree?'

'Course I do,' said Clive quickly.

'Well, that's something, I suppose. And what have you done towards finding out how the poor devil is, if anything?'

'I rung up and they're keeping him in until further notice.'

'Did they say how he is?' Don kept running his eyes over Clive as if he was going to do a drawing of him later. 'Did you ask them?'

'Yeah, they said he was as well as can be expected.'

'That just means he's not dead yet. Or he wasn't when you rung up. Which incidentally was how long ago?'

Clive thought. 'Hour. Hour and a half ago.'

'You get out there and give 'em another ring now. Go on.'

There was no use arguing, Clive knew. He went into the hall, which was just about big enough for an old-fashioned hallstand thing, a doormat, a potted plant with big dark shiny leaves and the foot of the stair. And the phone on a little table. Clive left the kitchen door open without thinking about it. That was Don's rule when he, Clive, was phoning – when he was phoning himself he kept it shut. Clive dialled. He already knew the hospital number.

While he was ringing he could hear his mother and Don talking in the kitchen, but only for a moment because Don, it must have been, kicked the door shut. Clive felt frightened, at least that was the closest he could get to how he felt – not frightened of what they might say at the hospital, well, he was, but separate. He could not have explained it to anyone. Perhaps he was scared of being the one who had killed the watchman or put him in a wheelchair. Yes, but not just of being punished for it. He wished the bloody hospital would answer and stop keeping him hanging about like this. Yeah, when he could be out driving his Porsche up the M1.

They answered, he asked for the ward, got a burst of some gooey ballet music and was put through. Mr Harris was as comfortable as could be expected. What name should they say? Just a friend, he told them.

He went back into the kitchen and reported. 'Still not dead, then,' said Don. 'Now, Clive, the way I look at it, your place is down at that hospital, but, er,' he half turned towards his wife, 'I'm told that's a bad idea.'

'He'd only be under their feet down there,' said Clive's mother. 'And not just that, he's the last person that fellow wants to be reminded of. Surely you can see that, Don.'

'I suppose I can.' Don nodded reluctantly. Giving way to that touch of opposition seemed to make him feel he could lash out a bit at Clive. 'If only you felt truly sorry for what you've done, there might be some hope for you.'

'I do feel sorry, Don.'

'Ay, you look it. Sorry you were nabbed, that's all. I suppose it was your mate's idea, was it, breaking into that joint?'

'No, it was mine.'

Don grinned sarcastically. 'Well, there's a change, I must say. Such honesty! But I don't see what you were after in there. You couldn't have hoped to get away with much stuff.'

'I didn't.' Now Clive felt he would say anything to get the heat off for a second. 'Just ten quid's worth of something. To pay Mum back. The money I stole out of her handbag.'

'Are you telling me you done that just so you could pay me back?' asked his mother in a funny hard voice. When he said yes, she got up and started to get the tea out.

'I see,' said Don, still grinning, 'so it's robbing Peter to pay Paul just after you finished robbing Paul. Oh, very neat. Cancels everything out, doesn't it? Well, it don't work with me, young Clive. Two wrongs don't make a right.' Don shut up for a moment, and when he went on he was back to the quieter manner he had shown when they started. 'You don't really know what I'm talking about, do you?' he said.

'I read you,' said Clive.

'Well, there's somebody as knows much more about these things than what I do, it's his job. I suppose he might do you some good, my lad – worth trying, any road. Mr Foster, the vicar. You owe him a call already.'

'Vicar? What do I owe him for?'

'He put up the money for your bail this morning,' said Don. 'I can't think why, but then I don't really know him more than to say hallo to. You go over and see him now and thank him for what he done.'

'I don't like the sound of that,' said Clive.

'One more reason for doing it. You've got to learn that life isn't just –'

Clive's mother cut in on her husband to say, 'Oh, Don, you were going to ring Bert before he goes out. Yes, you said to remind you you had to ring Bert.'

'Oh yeah, right, thanks, Alice. Well . . .'

When mother and son were alone, the mother said very coldly, 'Stop lying to me, Clive.'

'Sorry, Mum.'

'That's no good. Stop *lying*. Now as to that burglary thing, I don't know why you done it, I don't suppose you know yourself. Not thinking, as usual. Which doesn't mean I think you're just a thoughtless kid and what you do is all right with me because it's not. N-O-T, not. One day I might forgive you for what you done last night. I don't know. But I'll never forget it. You . . . you *thickhead*.'

Clive said nothing.

'Now you'd better go out the back way and go and see that vicar. Perhaps you'll speak the truth to him.'

4

Clive was glad enough to get out of the house, but he soon found he was a bit stuck when it came to finding the vicar. Still, he had the name, Foster, and he remembered seeing a church on the far side of the flyover where he could make a start. It could be Foster's own church, the one where he preached or whatever they did now, that was if a vicar stuck to just the one church. He could have a room or a flat in this one, or anyway, even if he had nothing to do with it, there should be somebody around who would probably know something. That was if it was open – perhaps it only opened on Sundays.

Anyway, here it was in front of him. Clive had been past new-looking buildings with signs on or near them that said they were this-or-that church but except for maybe a socking great cross on them they could have been new factories, with those up-and-down roofs and so on. But you could tell this one was a church a mile off, as Clive had, all separate, made of special stone and worked on a lot, different from other places. This one's sign said in old-fashioned gold lettering that it was St Christopher's Church.

There was a small door that was part of a bigger door and looked unfastened. When Clive tried a push, it opened easily and he stepped in – nobody could have said he was doing anything wrong. The instant silence inside reminded him of being in a church some time in the past, being taken to church, he could not remember how many times or how long ago or who had taken him. That was only for a second. Then he heard and saw enough to realize there was actually plenty going on, half a dozen people standing or walking about, equipment being moved or set up, audio equipment, microphones, loudspeakers, cables, a console, a cabinet. Remarks were going to and fro about volume, feedback, output. Clive had seen somewhere that some churches were being sold or converted into something else and wondered if this was one. He walked a few paces towards the action. Then one of the voices called out to him.

'Hallo there. Can I help you? Are you looking for me?' It was a lively, friendly voice.

Clive half turned round and saw somebody coming in his direction. 'Excuse me,' he said, 'I'm looking for the . . .' He had been going to ask about the vicar but stopped.

A fellow of about thirty came up to him, tallish, serious-looking but with a nice smile. 'Do you want me?' he asked. 'I'm Robin Foster. And I know who you are – you're Clive Rayner. I saw you in court this morning. Welcome.' And he stuck out his hand.

Clive could not help hesitating for a second before he put out his own hand and shook. 'Pleased to meet you,' he said in a hurry. 'Sorry, I didn't realize . . .'

'Good to see you, Clive,' said this offbeat sort of vicar. 'I've been more or less expecting you, you know.'

'Oh,' said Clive, still not clear about what was going on. 'I thought I'd come along and, er, say thank you for paying that money at the court so they let me out after whatever it was.'

'No thanks needed,' said Foster. 'Glad to do it.'

'But what I don't see is how you knew about me, like. So quick. And paying the money, or perhaps vicars always do that, do they?'

In the last half-minute, Foster had been leading Clive over to the end of what Clive remembered was called a pew and they sat down in it side by side.

'As to how I know,' said Foster slowly, not taking his eyes off Clive, 'let's just say I make it my business to keep fairly closely in touch with what goes on in my parish, particularly as regards, let's say younger people. Call it investing in the future, if you like.'

Clive had no idea what the last bit meant, but he nodded his head.

'And I *paid the money* because, well, it sounds rather old-fashioned, probably, but anyway I see it as my sacred duty to help those in trouble.' Foster sounded very serious when he went on, 'And you're in trouble, Clive.'

This time Clive understood all right, or he thought he did. 'Yeah, I know I am,' he said.

'I may be able to help you further, if you want to be helped,' said Foster, and looked at his watch. 'I bring you a short message.'

'Who from?'

'From God,' said Foster. He had rather big, very clear eyes, Clive noticed.

Just then, a bloke appeared who looked exactly the kind of bloke nobody would expect to find in a church from the top of his teased blue hair to his red running shoes, one of the lot with the audio equipment that Clive had completely forgotten about ever since the vicar turned up. The bloke was carrying a microphone stand and said in a voice like a baby, 'Where do you want this, Robin?'

Foster said a bit crossly, 'Don't ask me, Shawn – the group should be here any moment – wait and ask them. All right. Sorry about all this, Clive,' he said when the blue-haired bloke had gone.

'Er, that's okay, vicar. What's it all in aid of, then?'

'We're putting on a little poetry-and-rock. Just to see how it goes.'

Another bit that took some getting hold of. 'Rock? In a church?'

'Most certainly in a church,' said Foster, going into some sort of routine. 'Why not? It's part of the tradition. The church belongs to the people, Clive, and the people want their own music, the music of their own time. I'm afraid religion's a living force, Clive, and it changes as the times change, like all living things. But I mustn't bore you with my liturgical theories.'

Holding it there was about right – he was just starting to lose Clive, who had kept up pretty well so far, considering, and now made what he hoped was a polite face. 'But, er, what about this message?' he asked.

'Ah, yes. Now. God wants you to –'

There was a hell of a squeaking or creaking where somebody was getting feedback from an amplifier or something. The vicar hurried over and did some ticking-off, and in a minute he and Clive went into a little room up to one side, where there was a tall writing-desk with an inkstand thing on it and a couple of big books in worn leather covers. On the way there they had passed near a granny-type of about eighty kneeling in a corner and wiping her tears with a handkerchief.

'There's one that's not going to care for the rock much,' said Clive.

'We won't be disturbed in here . . . What? Who?'

'That old girl out there.'

'Oh, yes. No. She has her own path to God. Apologizing for something, asking for something – how would I know?'

Clive decided to let that one go for now.

'Right, let's get down to business. It was your stepfather's idea that you came to see me, wasn't it? He pressurized you? Yes, I thought as much. I recognized the type as soon as I set eyes on him. I'm afraid our Mr MacIntyre isn't what I'd call much of a Christian.'

Clive felt that would do very well to be going on with. 'Oh, he's not?'

'Let me describe him to you, Clive. Here goes. Gloomy, no sense of humour, working-class Tory voter, sure he's in the right, mean with the cash, dead stubborn, always on about evil and wrong-doing. How's that?'

'You just took his picture,' said Clive, almost beaming.

Foster said, 'Thirty years ago he'd have been threatening you with hell-fire.'

'He come pretty near that already.'

They grinned together for a minute, then Foster turned really serious. 'Now, Clive,' he said, folding his arms. 'You and your mate, young Terry, you went and broke into Butterfields', never mind why. The night-watchman came at you, and you hit out at him, on the spur of the moment, by instinct, without thinking. He got hurt, but you didn't mean him to get hurt, you had no intention of hurting him, correct?'

'Well, that bit is,' said Clive, 'but I –'

'And you were caught,' – Foster was going on steadily like a judge – 'and you're going to pay the penalty. In fact you're paying some of it already. Oh yes, you are, whether you know it or not. I don't mean the legal penalty, I mean the penalty – inside you. You feel ashamed. You're sorry for what you did *and* you feel ashamed. As that stepfather of yours would put it, you feel you've sinned.'

Clive just said, 'Well . . .' but he nearly said yes.

'You did wrong, you know you did wrong, and you're sorry. You repent, Clive. As it used to be called. And that means – God has forgiven you. That's the message I was talking about. But that's not the end of it. Now, your task, your sacred duty is to learn to forgive yourself, to get rid of those feelings of shame. Until you do, Clive,' said Foster, 'you'll be in serious trouble, as I said.'

'Serious trouble?' repeated Clive, feeling baffled again. 'But I thought the trouble you were talking about . . .'

'And that's where your stepfather comes in. A very dangerous man, our friend Don MacIntyre.'

'Oh no, vicar, you're wrong there,' said Clive straight away. 'He's never raised his hand to me. He wouldn't, not with my mum –'

'No no, I mean dangerous to your state of mind in your present situation. He'll go on trying to fill you with shame and a sense of sin and misery. And that isn't what God wants for any human soul, which ought to be filled with light and love and peace.' He was gazing at Clive, almost as if he was daring him to laugh. 'Forgive yourself, my son, and be healed.'

Something in particular had been bothering Clive and now he tried to come out with it. 'Look, Reverend –'

'Robin,' said Foster, still seriously.

'Look, er, I didn't actually clobber that watchman. I was just trying to get away from him, like, and he went and fell over this rail thing and hurt himself. I know it don't make no difference, but still, you know.'

'Oh, indeed I do know, and it makes a lot of difference. If that stands up in court you're bound to get off more lightly.'

'No, I didn't mean about the law, I meant it don't make no difference to how bad it was, what I done, because the bloke'd never have hurt himself if I hadn't of broke in, see? I mean you do see, don't you?'

While Clive was speaking there was the sound of voices from outside, from the main part of the church. Somebody seemed to be arriving. Foster turned his head a couple of inches, then turned it back again.

'Oh, forget it, Clive,' he said, looking at his watch. 'You did wrong, you're sorry, *really* sorry, you're forgiven, as I explained to you, and that should be the end of it between yourself and God. He gave you your life to live it and enjoy it to the full extent of which you're capable. This isn't 1950, you know.'

Clive was frowning to himself, wondering. 'You don't sort of *blame* me, do you?' he said slowly.

'Well.' Foster clasped his hands together and said, 'I think you've been foolish, and thoughtless, and irresponsible, but to me you're just another human being. I certainly don't blame you. Who am I to do that?'

Now Clive wondered even more. 'Who are *you*?' he said, and stopped. 'Anyway, thank you,' – he had been going to really try to say Robin, but found he could just not manage it – 'very much for, er, talking to me. I'll be off now.'

'Wouldn't you like to stay for our run-through?'

'No, I'd better be getting back,' said Clive. 'Er, good evening.'

'Cheers, Clive,' said the vicar. 'God bless you, mate.'

Clive nodded and smiled and found his way back to the door he had come in by. He realized he had been half expecting to hear the music starting up just as he went out, but all he heard was a huge sweep of notes and a voice shouting something in what sounded like a foreign language.

5

For the rest of that evening Clive stayed out of the way, and the next morning he kept his head down till he heard Don go off to work. In the kitchen his mother boiled an egg for him and made fresh tea. While she did this, she told him about the funny old girl in Westbourne Grove she was going to clean for that morning, or actually more to gossip with. She was showing Clive that she and he were still completely on speaking terms, even though there was a lot left to be thrashed out between them. Just as she was leaving, his mother told him to be sure to be in at four o'clock, because a woman from the Town Hall was coming round to see them, all three of them.

'What sort of woman?' Clive felt uneasy straight away.

'I don't know, some social worker, I gathered. She rang last night. Now you be here, my lad.'

'Don't worry, Mum.'

'Unless you want to be discussed behind your back. Oh, did you get that vicar?'

'Yeah. Nice guy, sort of. Bit young, I thought he was.'

'Well, that's not a crime, is it? Just as well for some. I must be off – tell me about it later.'

Clive got through the day somehow with television, some not very new audio tapes and a horror video he knew by heart by now, even the ordinary bits, but it cost him nothing because the fellow whose van it had come out of had got himself nicked. He took a free lunch off the pizza parlour in return for clearing up some of the muck afterwards and was ready and waiting in his bedroom at four right on the button, like a bloody paratrooper standing by for the drop, he thought to himself. He could hear the other two downstairs, gassing away as ever. When the doorbell rang he dived straight for the kitchen and was sitting next to his mother when Don fetched the Town Hall woman in and said she was called Miss Adams.

The next bit went rather like the kind of TV show Clive sometimes saw a couple of minutes of before the programme he wanted came on – a sort of panel, with the Adams woman bringing the experts in one after the other. While Don was giving her a dose of his views on this and that, Clive looked her over. She was young too, like the vicar, not bad looking but not fanciable either, not dolled up but not dowdy, and serious, still like the vicar only more so, more full-time. She was listening to the usual tripe from Don as though he was some famous professor on about his big discovery.

'I quite *understand*, Mr MacIntyre,' said Miss Adams. 'Of *course* you have to do your duty as Clive's stepfather.' She leant pretty hard on about one word in every dozen. 'Or what you see as your duty.'

'I don't reckon as I need anybody from the Town Hall coming in here and lecturing me on my duty,' said Don, about as easy-going as if he had been talking about a bump-up in the price of draught bitter.

'We all have our beliefs and it's our duty to act on them.' There was a bit of Wales in the way she talked, it struck Clive. 'Up to a point, that is. But we mustn't be *rigid* about them.'

'Rigid?' said Don, sort of peering at the word.

'What I mean is, Mr MacIntyre, that there's got to be some *flexibility*. Circumstances alter cases, if you like.'

'Oh, they do, do they? A crime's a crime, and there's no circumstances I can imagine that'll alter that case. That's according to my belief.'

Don was starting to warm up now, to get into his part, and it was looking as if a nice little set-to was on the way, but then Clive's mother put her oar in.

'Don,' she said, smiling at him, 'you know I'm with you, love, but you remember we did agree we'd listen to what Miss Adams had to say. You know. Give her a fair hearing, at least.'

'Ay, we did that, Alice, but I think I've listened to enough to know what's coming next. Clive's only a young lad, says she. We mustn't expect too much of him when all's said and done. Like keeping the law. Well, I've no patience with that kind of guff.'

'Don – *get* some patience for God's sake. Miss Adams has come here to help us. She's on our side.'

'That's a very sensible attitude, Mrs MacIntyre,' said the Adams woman.

'Lot of bloody rubbish if you ask me,' said Don, starting to hit the table.

'Nobody's asking you,' said Clive's mother. 'Now you and I had better take ourselves off and let Miss Adams talk to Clive alone.'

Don objected, and quite outspoken he was about it, but it was no use with the two women on the same side, something anybody could have seen coming, Clive reckoned, and in half a minute this social worker had him to herself. She got more relaxed and friendly straight away.

'Do you smoke?' she asked Clive, and offered him a Marlboro.

'Oh, ta,' he said, and lit her cigarette and felt a charlie doing it. That was probably the idea, with her being the sort who read books on psychology.

'Now, Clive, I'd better just quickly explain what I'm doing here.' Miss Adams wore glasses, but the frames were obviously not National Health. 'While you and Terry are on remand, various people are up to various things. The police'll be preparing their case, but you and I, we needn't worry about that – I'm nothing to do with them. What *my* job is, I'm gathering material, information, for a report on your home background, your family situation, and your own – what sort of person you are. One of my colleagues is setting up a similar dialogue with Terry.'

'What are you supposed to be doing all this for?' asked Clive.

'It'll be *evidence* when your case comes up for trial. Don't you see? Look, Clive, suppose you were – sick, mentally disturbed; we've no reason as yet to believe you are,' said Miss Adams, not smiling or anything, 'but let's suppose you were. Now obviously that'd make a difference in court, wouldn't it? They'd have to take that into consideration.'

'Yeah, I reckon they would.' Well, thought Clive, nobody could say she went at things too fast.

'Well then, *other* points can make a difference too. Your stepfather, he's pretty hard on you, isn't he?'

'Yeah,' said Clive, only stating a fact.

'And your mother tends to take your side, I suppose?'

'Well – sometimes she does. Not automatic-like, though.'

'I'm sure she does *typically*,' said Miss Adams, smiling now for a second. 'Now that puts you in a conflict situation right away. We'll have to go into that later in depth; this is just an exploratory session.'

'Oh – yeah.' Clive reckoned he was fielding the long words pretty well.

Miss Adams puffed on her cigarette like someone who had taken up smoking just the other day. She said, quieter than before, 'Clive, what about your father? Your real father.'

'I know who you mean. He went off. Married somebody else.'

'Was he hard on you too?' asked Miss Adams, opening the turnover notepad on the table in front of her.

'No. He was very kind. He used to . . .' Clive stopped speaking because he had suddenly thought it had been his father who had taken him to church that time, or those times, when he was small, but found he could not say that or anything else just for a moment.

Miss Adams had noticed nothing. She wrote on her notepad and said, '*Another* conflict situation. Do you ever see him?'

'I did pretty regular, till they went to Canada a couple of years back.'

'Deprivation situation,' said Miss Adams. 'I expect you miss him a lot?'

'Sometimes,' said Clive. 'When I get a letter mostly.'

'I expect you often wish you lived with him, your father, instead of here.'

'Well, it does sound good there, but no, not really. I like being with my mum.'

Muttering something about what sounded to him like a possible mother fixation, Miss Adams said, 'Tell me, Clive – what was in your *mind* when you and Terry went off to break into Butterfields'?'

'Nothing much, really. I was in a mood. Don, my stepfather, he'd been banging on at me. Because . . .'

Clive made himself finish. 'Because I'd taken some cash out of Mum's handbag.'

Miss Adams muttered something about that was consistent, then said out loud, 'I see. Now let's get on, shall we?'

'Get *on*? On to what?' Clive was puzzled again. 'Don't you want to know any more about me nicking the cash? Why I took it and that?'

'That can wait. It's not significant. What I *do* want to know is this – how do you feel *now*, Clive? About the break-in and the rest of it.'

'Oh. I don't know. Bit rotten. Fed up. You know, sort of . . .'

'Guilty?' asked Miss Adams with her head on one side.

'Yeah. Guilty. That's right. Why not? I am guilty, aren't I?'

'No you're *not*, Clive.' She sounded very firm.

He was astonished now. '*What?* What do you mean? They want me to *plead* guilty in court, for God's sake.'

'That's nothing to *do* with it!'

'Nothing to do with it? Bloody hell, I done it, and I say I done it, and they take my word for it. I mean who else is there?'

'Clive, please, this is all just semantics, you know. It's not the *point*.'

'All right,' he said, 'I'm beaten,' and he felt it, but sort of angry too. 'You tell me what the point is, Miss Adams.'

'In any meaningful sense,' she led off, '*you*, Clive

Rayner, are not guilty of anything at all. Anything relevant, anything that really matters. It's society that's guilty, the system and the people who live off it and in it and around it. We all made it happen. We are all guilty.'

When he had heard that, and had taken it in as much as he could or was ever going to, and had realized there was no more to come for a couple of seconds, he really for once in his life wanted to do something violent, only he could not imagine what. Thinking he must sound like a robot, he said, 'Would you like a cup of tea, Miss Adams?'

'No thank you, love.' She lit herself another cigarette, blew out smoke and said, 'Now, just try looking at it this way, Clive. You're a *casualty*, you're a *victim*, you've been neglected and deprived, you're the child of a broken home, you're in a conflict situation with your stepfather . . .'

Clive interrupted. 'That don't go for Terry, none of it. His parents get on a treat and they think the world of him.'

'Through no fault of your own,' she went on as if he had stayed sitting there with his mouth shut, 'you've got these unanswered needs for attention and understanding that nobody's done anything about. What you did wasn't a criminal act, any of it, except technically – it was a cry for *help*. Mind you, Clive, to be quite honest, we're not out of the wood yet. *We* know you didn't mean any harm to Mr Harris, but, well, it doesn't look too good, that side of it, I'm afraid.'

'What? The watchman bloke? What about him, what's happened?' Clive spoke in a jumble. He was full of fear.

'You have heard, have you?'

'Heard what? They wouldn't tell me nothing at the hospital.'

'Well . . . something to do with his spinal cord. He may not be able to walk, anyway not for a time. They don't know for certain yet.'

'When will they know?' Now Clive was horrified. 'What are his chances?'

'You mustn't blame yourself, Clive. It was an *accident*. You didn't *want* it to happen, of course, but there we are, it did. Let's get on.'

Miss Adams turned over a page of her notepad and asked him something about his childhood, but he had stopped listening.

6

The next day, Clive went and got a job at the supermarket pushing trolleys back from the car-park and sweeping out. He got it not because he wanted to work or fancied any part of what he had to do, but because doing it and having all those people around helped him not to think about what Miss Adams had said, and what she might say at their next session that evening, and how that watchman bloke, Harris, was doing in the hospital, and everything else. He arranged to see Terry and the two birds later at the Bengal Light, not because he was exactly mad about seeing any of them, but because the thought of it was going to help him not to start thinking that Miss Adams was always going to be there, asking her questions and coming out with those ideas of hers he found so hard to believe or even to understand.

When she had gone, and he had just managed to get out of being given a lift to the Indian joint in her car, and he was walking along the side of the flyover approach, Clive felt marvellously free for about five seconds, before the whole thing closed in on him again. He was early, so he hung about for a bit in the Parade, looking into the windows of shops that sold sideboards and lawnmowers and keen stuff like that. After enough of that he was still too early, because when he looked in the eatery door there was Paula on her own, and he felt like ducking out again, but she had seen him.

'Hallo,' she said when he sat down opposite her, and went on reading the evening paper she had brought, as though they were a couple of people sitting in a train.

That was fine with Clive, or as fine as it was going to get. Having her there on her own was bad enough, but nothing to having to talk to her. He got them lagers. Then he saw a middle-aged bloke and wife at a table across the way looking at them and then discussing them. They probably thought he had it off with Paula every night regular and twice on Sundays. That was a laugh, that was. He remembered the ridiculous grab he had made that time at Terry's when his folks were out, and how she had jumped a foot in the air and told him to keep his bloody hands to himself and not to try that again ever. A relief really. Why did he still see her, have her around, ask her out? Because it was what you did.

Just then Paula read out a bit from the paper in her stupid peevish way, something about Tube fares going up, and he ticked her off. That shut her up for a minute, but then the same thing happened again, this time over something about some pub somewhere going to come down, and he ticked her off again and serve her right. She glared at him, and he thought she might have been going to slap him, in which case darling had better hang on to her front teeth. But she calmed down quicker than usual and said, 'What's up, lover-boy?'

'Eh?' he grunted.

'Look,' she said, 'I know you're worried about this court case thing on Thursday, but there's no need to be bloody horrible to me because of it.'

'I'm not,' said Clive.

'Yes you are, mate, you've been bloody horrible ever since you came in.'

'Listen, I didn't say I hadn't been bloody horrible to you, I said I wasn't worried about the bloody court case.'

'Oh yeah.' She frowned. 'Why not?'

Might as well talk about it as anything else, he decided. She had folded up the paper and was set on a natter anyway. 'All cut and dried, ennit,' he said. 'I plead guilty and everybody gets up one after the other and says well, considering everything I been through it's a miracle I didn't go and blow up the bloody warehouse, and I get off with a year or two's probation and a fine. The end.'

'How do you know?'

'Apparently that's what the solicitor bloke was saying. My solicitor. I'm seeing him in his office tomorrow. He's free, did you know that?'

'Free?' said Paula in the way Clive had expected, thick and fed-up with it.

'Free. No charge. Zero cost. To me. Legal Aid they call it.'

Paula frowned again. She said, 'If you're not worried about the court case, why are you being bloody horrible to me, then?'

'How would you feel if there was a fellow who couldn't walk because of you?'

'Accident, wasn't it?' said Paula, looking over Clive's shoulder towards the door. 'You couldn't help it. Didn't mean it.'

'How would you feel,' he said, wondering why he was bothering, 'if you was driving a car, see, and a guy who's been boozing his bloody head off comes out of nowhere and falls in front of you and you run him over and they have to take his legs off.'

'But you broke into that warehouse. Not like just driving a car.'

'Never mind that side of it. You're driving the car, this bloke falls in front of you.'

'You mean, you mean like it was his fault and not mine?'

'Yes!' said Clive, trying not to shout. 'Yes.'

'All right.' Frown. 'Well, you know, if it was *all* this fellow's fault, I don't know. I'd feel sorry for him, course I would, like I'd feel sorry for anyone.'

'Like you'd feel sorry for anyone and that's it.'

'Anyone with no legs.'

'I get you,' said Clive. He went on with what he had

been thinking about why he still had Paula around. Because you were supposed to have a bird around, right. Just any old bird? No, a sort of suitable one, one that suited you, whether you knew it or not. So this one suited him. And what did that make him?

It was a bit of luck that Terry and Marilyn came along just then, chattering, apologizing for being late, calling for menus. Paula cheered up at seeing Marilyn, the only person there she really wanted to see, Clive realized. But Terry seemed to have noticed something.

'What's the matter, sunshine?' he asked Clive after a minute. 'I smell bad tonight?'

'It's not you, Terry,' said Paula. 'He's been –'

Clive broke in, '– bloody awful to her ever since I turned up.'

'He's worried about this court case whatever he says,' said Paula.

'I am not repeat not worried about this perishing court case!' said Clive. 'It's this night-watchman fellow – Harris.'

'Yeah, I heard,' said Terry, looking round for the waiter. 'Bloody bad luck, that was.'

Marilyn said, 'He'll get, you know, they'll pay him something, his firm or the judge or somebody.'

'Oh, terrific,' said Clive. 'Good as a brand-new pair of legs.'

'Cool it, Clive,' said Terry.

'If you're so worked up about him,' said Paula, 'why don't you go and see him or something?'

'I am not worked up. I can't go and see him.' Clive

looked round at the others. 'Well, something about I might go and say something, like tell him it was my fault, and you're not meant to do that. I don't get it, but the solicitor, he'd know, wouldn't he?'

Nobody contradicted him. Then Terry said to Clive, 'You been seeing one of these social workers?'

'Yeah, twice already and again Wednesday. I've got her up to here. Told me she'd been asking about me at my school and everywhere. Female called Miss Adams. No, Tel, nothing like that, you haven't seen her. Anyway, according to her I'm in a conflict situation, maybe a couple. What's yours been on about?'

'Mine's a fellow,' said Terry. 'Well, first he went on about me being insecure, but he couldn't find out why I should be. So he forgot that, and the way it landed up, I got a weak personality and you talked me into it.'

'Well, I did, didn't I?' said Clive.

'That's right. Well, I didn't need much talking, I was a mug. Where is that bloody waiter? I'm starving.'

'So'm I,' said Paula and Marilyn together.

The waiter got there and there was more chatter, about prawn biriani and chicken something else and chapattis, and after a bit Clive joined in.

The only other thing worth mentioning before the case came up happened about tea-time on the Wednesday, when Clive was coming back from the supermarket. He was just getting to the point where he stepped off the walkway when he heard and almost felt a car going the same way slow down and pull in right behind him, just like on the afternoon of the day all this carry-on started. Clive knew who it was. He stopped and turned round and there was that Sergeant Parnell in the police car with his window rolled down. This time, instead of getting out he spoke from his seat for the moment.

'Hallo there, Clive, hallo again,' he said in the put-on friendly tone Clive remembered. 'Message for you. You're required to attend the Borough Court tomorrow at ten a.m. That's ten o'clock in the morning to you. Got it?'

Clive ignored the sarcasm. 'Why d'you come to tell me that?' he asked.

'Oh, we find it helps all round to give these little informal reminders. Saves the court's time, which is more valuable than ours, of course.'

'No,' said Clive, 'I meant, why'd *you* come? You could just have sent one of your stooges, couldn't you?'

'I happened to be passing, that's all.'

'Yeah?' Clive took out a cigarette and lit it. 'Well, now you've passed, why don't you pass off?'

The sergeant gave a genuine grin, a nasty one. 'You ought to be cutting down on those, sonny. They won't be so easy to come by where you're going tomorrow. I'd advise you to start tapering off now.'

A lorry roared by on the approach road and Clive waited a few seconds before answering. 'You don't scare me, Sergeant Parnell,' he said, blowing smoke towards the police car.

'Really? I'll have to try a bit harder then, won't I?'

Moving as if they had been practising it, the sergeant and the constable called Jack jumped out of the car. Without actually touching Clive, the sergeant backed him to the edge of the grassy slope, so that if he went back another pace he might stagger or slip.

'Bit of news for you, Clive. Quite a little nugget. Until a few hours ago I was very down in the mouth about your chances. Everybody seemed to love you, including the chief of my division, who'll be speaking for the police in court. He believes in sensitive policing. One of those caring coppers, you know – I care too, of course, but about different things. Well, then I happened to run across someone who doesn't like you at all. A Mrs Harris. Wife of the chap you didn't push off that staircase.'

'What can she do?' asked Clive, trying to play it cool.

'Oh, she and her husband can instruct his solicitor to lay great stress on Mr Harris's condition and your moral responsibility for it, and ask the court to show its concern and disapproval by awarding a considerably heavier sentence than it might otherwise have done in view of your youth, almost stainless record, psychological condition etcetera, etcetera.'

'What sort of sentence?'

The sergeant's manner turned hard for the first time. 'Yes, that's what bothers you, isn't it? – nothing else. What sort of sentence? Inside. Somewhere. Somewhere not very nice at all. Six months. Maybe a year. Maybe longer. Not my decision – it's out of my hands. It's never been *in* my hands, I'm sorry to say.'

'But it'd be borstal, not prison,' said Clive, trying now to keep his voice from trembling. 'I'm too young for prison.'

'Oh, well it's called something else now,' said the sergeant, relaxed again. 'To make the caring classes think it's nicer than borstal. But it isn't really. It's still not at all nice. Because that's not the idea. Now you watch a lot of television, don't you, Clive, you must have a fair idea of it from the documentaries and so on. There was a play about it a few weeks ago. Very well produced, I thought. One of the inmates knocked himself off because of what some of the other inmates had been doing to him. Very true to life, my colleagues tell me. Yes. Well, we'll be getting along now. No rest for the wicked.'

Clive made a last effort. He nodded over at the constable, who was leaning against the car a few feet away. 'Your boy there, what's he standing to attention for, or doesn't he know?'

'Don't make me come and show you, son,' said the constable. 'Don't tempt me, all right?'

'Off you go now,' said the sergeant. 'Back home.'

It was no use – Clive stood his ground for a moment or two, then turned round and went away down the slope towards the row of houses. When he looked back, the two policemen were still there, watching him.

*

Clive found some of the court proceedings hard to follow. They were almost nothing like what he had seen on TV and he had no idea who half the people were or what they were trying to get across, except a lot of detail about stuff he knew nothing about. He recognized Miss Adams all right, though he kept having trouble recognizing the fellow she was talking about as himself. He tried to go along by looking miserable and deprived and a terrible victim of everything. But almost right off, never mind the flannel, he found he could tell roughly that things were going to go the way Miss Adams and the solicitor had said they would, and not the way that bloody cop had said. Mrs Harris, the watchman's wife, seemed to have stayed at home.

So it was probation for Clive and Terry, and a fine of £100 for Clive because he had been the ringleader. Foster the vicar was sitting in the public part, and when they got to the bit about the fine he waved to Clive and winked and did a thumbs-up, so it looked as if that part was taken care of. Then suddenly it was all over, and they had got off lightly, and Clive could simply not understand why he felt so little different when everybody else was laughing and jabbering as if they had won the pools.

Clive's mother hugged him and told him it was marvellous. 'All that worrying gone for nothing. All water under the bridge. What a relief. Thank God.' She was crying a little and wiping the tears away with her fingers. 'You'll have to do what the probation officer tells you, mind,' she threw in after a bit, but there was not much to be seen just then of the tough character who had called him ignorant and a thick-head.

Paula was next. She ran up and gave Clive a smacking kiss full on the lips, and held on to him, and for a moment he was surprised and chuffed, thinking to himself she cared after all, she really minded, until he got the nasty thought that maybe it had more to do with grabbing a piece of the limelight. 'Let's go out tonight and celebrate,' she said. 'Not that Indian joint again – somewhere special. I'll think where.'

By this time they were in the hall with marble and pillars outside the courtroom and everyone was there at once. Clive and Terry did a big handshake and a bit of a dance. They both remembered just in time to thank the solicitor. Miss Adams came over, and Clive was wondering whether he would have to kiss her or what, but she solved the problem by going into a sort of French-general thing with arms round each other but not quite touching faces. Terry got the same treatment, he saw.

'Just part of the service,' she said, looking quite pink in the face. 'But I'm relying on you not to let me down in the future. You too, Terry.'

'You bet we won't,' said Terry, very reliable.

'Do our best,' said Clive. 'Can't do more.'

His mother looked at him and then asked, 'Aren't you pleased, love? You must be. But you don't . . . seem to be.'

'Yeah, I'm pleased,' said Clive, 'course I am. Pleased

not to be going to whatever they call borstal now. Who wants to go there? Course I'm pleased.'

'What's the matter, then?' said Paula with a touch of her old peeve.

'I can't talk to you,' said Clive. 'Hang on a minute.'

He hurried over to the sergeant and constable who were crossing the hall towards the street doors. If they had been in court he had not seen them. When he called out to them they stopped and turned.

'Ah, the young victim of society,' said the sergeant with a smile, 'I was nearly crying in there, you know, at the thought of what we'd all done to you. You're lucky not to be a raving lunatic, Clive.'

Clive said, 'That woman – Mrs Harris, the one you said was going to get me sent down – what happened to her?'

'Oh well, somebody must have persuaded her to change her mind, mustn't they, or change her tune. We often find that with this sort of case, don't we, Jack?'

'Who persuaded her?' asked Clive. 'What for? Change her tune?'

'Wheels within wheels, sonny. Anyway, what do you care? In a manner of speaking, the good lady got you off.'

'What does *he* think, the watchman bloke?'

'No idea, Clive. Why don't you go and ask him yourself? It'd be quite safe for you to go and talk to him, now the case is all over and done with.'

The two policemen seemed in no hurry to leave. 'Listen,' said Clive, 'you knew when you stopped me on the road yesterday it was going to go the way it's gone, didn't you?'

'We never think of a case as certain until it's officially closed.'

'Do we, Jack?' sneered Clive. 'No, we don't, sergeant. *You* knew, as good as, didn't you?'

'Yes,' said Sergeant Parnell. 'I deliberately misled you.'

'What for? It didn't do you any good. What was the idea?'

'I have answered three questions and that is enough. Don't you think so? Clive? The idea was to give you a bad time, the only sort of bad time I could manage. And don't say "what for?" again, or I'll have to start thinking you're stupid. As I told you down at the station on the night of your "lark", I wanted to punish you. One, because criminals deserve to be punished. Two, for my own personal satisfaction. And three, because punishment's good for the soul. Your soul in this case.'

'You got a big bang out of this, didn't you?' said Clive. 'You been having a ball with me, all the way along. Laughing your head off.'

'Our Clive should be in the social worker business himself, shouldn't he, Jack? Quite the little psychologist.'

'I'd prefer a shorter word, sergeant.'

'Bloody fascists,' said Clive.

It was all he could think of to say, but the policemen seemed to agree heartily. 'That's it, you've got it,' said the sergeant with another smile, and the constable nodded his head and did a sort of slaphappy salute. Turning to go, the sergeant went on, 'Well, my colleague and I have got to get after someone else who's had a raw deal from society. Poor devil went for his wife with a sledgehammer. Goodbye, Clive. For now. I'll be seeing you.'

The two policemen went to the street doors, where they politely stood aside for Terry, Marilyn and Terry's parents to leave. Terry saw Clive as he was going and waved and called.

'So long, Clive. See you tonight.'

Clive waved back and went over to his own lot again. His feet felt as if they weighed a ton.

Trying not to smile too much with affection and relief, his mother said, 'Clive, I don't think I've heard you thank Miss Adams for everything she done. You'd have been in very deep water without her, I hope you realize.'

'Oh, I do. Don't I know it.' Clive was trying to do what his mother wanted, including not screaming his head off with frustration and hopelessness and boredom. 'Yeah. Well, thank you very much, Miss Adams, for everything you done.'

'You're more than welcome – I'm here to help people,' she said, looking at him seriously through her glasses.

Don, in a sort of dark-grey suit that had gone a bit shiny here and there, had to have his say. 'By rights I ought to be saying thank you too, Miss Adams. It's only decent, after all. No man wants to see his family brought to disgrace and grief. I've no wish to have anyone suffer, not just like that, but that's not the end of it – there's a fellow down in that hospital who can't walk because a boy here broke the law, and don't you nor anybody else try and tell me – no no, please, both of you,' he said desperately when he saw his wife and Miss Adams getting ready to shut him up or walk him away – 'please listen, this is very important. A crime's been committed and people are going on as if somebody's won a prize. You can't wipe out a crime but you can do something, call it what it is, it's a *crime*, for God's sake. If you'd only pay attention . . .'

He gave up. The two women had been looking to and fro at each other, and Miss Adams said, 'Nobody's trying to *deny* there's been a crime committed, Mr MacIntyre. After all, we've been attending a court of *justice* . . .'

Clive slipped away.

7

The people at the hospital seemed to be trying to choke Clive off at first, but when he told them he had just been fined and put on probation for breaking into the place where Mr Harris had been hurt, they showed him up straight away. Then he thought at first he had been taken to the wrong place, because in the little room at the end of the ward there was an empty unmade bed and a rough-looking auntie type sitting on a stool. She gave him a dirty look.

'Mr Harris?' said Clive, feeling a total twit.

'Gone down to X-ray. I'm his wife. Who are you?'

'My name's Clive Rayner. I'm the fellow who –'

'I know who you are. And I know what you done and you ought to pay for it. You ought to be in prison, you ought. And if I had my way you would be. I was going to do my best to see you was put there, I promise you. But that Stone, he talked me out of it.'

'Stone?' If it was a name it meant nothing to Clive.

'Solicitor bloke come in yesterday. Talked me and

Arthur out of having the accident discussed in court, says the firm wouldn't be so generous if we did. Generous, he called it. Then he couldn't get Arthur to say you pushed him off of the stairs, because he wouldn't tell a lie, not Arthur, and that Stone says that queers our pitch for a grant from the Compensation Board people. So what with everything, me and Arthur, we won't be getting much.'

Clive made nothing to speak of out of most of this either, but he could tell Mrs Harris was too angry to care. He started to babble about having no cash himself but she soon cut in.

'Where would you get your hands on any cash, bar out of a blind man's tin? No, what I said, you ought to pay by going to prison. Funny thing, you read in the paper about all the prisons being overcrowded, but when someone comes along as really deserves a stretch, like . . .' To Clive's amazement, Mrs Harris suddenly stopped talking for a moment and went on almost as if she was apologizing. 'I been so upset . . . I couldn't help it . . .'

He had the sense to keep quiet at that, and a moment later a hospital attendant came pushing a trolley thing into the room with Harris on it. There was a nurse there too and a youngish bloke who was probably a doctor. Between them they got Harris, who seemed pretty much laid out flat, back on to his bed and tucked up and the doctor had a bit to say.

'There is a further very small improvement,' he told them in a kind sort of voice, 'but I must make it quite clear to you both that this process might well not continue, or not continue very far. I can't say whether it will or not. Nobody could. To be honest, all we can do is hope.' Harris thanked him and he went out, nodding at Clive, maybe taking him for a nephew or something.

Harris turned his head towards Clive. 'What do you want here?'

'I would have come before, Mr Harris,' said Clive, 'but my solicitor said I definitely mustn't.'

'But he reckons it's safe now, eh? Ah, they're all the same. Anyway, why've you come now?'

'See how you are,' said Clive.

'Well, you can see.'

'He might be like he is for the rest of his life,' said Mrs Harris. 'You heard what that doctor said.'

'What are the chances?' asked Clive.

'There's just no telling,' said Harris. 'They've said that all along, and I believe them. I trust them.'

'So now you know you can be off,' said his wife.

Clive said in a rush, 'I come to say I'm sorry. It sounds dead ridiculous, I can see that. It's what you say when you tread on a fellow's foot. But I can't think of no other way. I'm sorry you're hurt so bad. I'm sorry you're hurt at all – you hadn't done nothing to me. I'm sorry I went and broke into that place. Because none of it would have happened if I hadn't of done that.' Mrs Harris started to say something, but Clive went straight on talking to Harris, slower now. 'I want *you* to know that *I* know that. They all say it was an accident, and it was, but you got to have something to make an accident happen. And that was me, me breaking in, what made it happen. It *might* have happened some other way, sure, but it didn't. It happened *that* way. Because of me.' Mrs Harris said a bit more there, but again the other two took no notice. 'I'm sorry. If there was anything I could do I'd do it, more than willing, but I been over it a dozen times in my mind and I just can't think of nothing. Nothing at all.'

Mrs Harris said, 'What do you want with us?' and this time they heard her.

Over the previous few days, Clive had had some practice in finding words for his feelings, but he was still not much good at it. 'I just want to tell you,' he said, took a couple of breaths and finished up, 'to tell you I know it's all because of me.'

'You want us to say we don't hold it against you,' said Mrs Harris straight out, not asking a question.

That bit at least Clive was quite clear about. 'No!' he said loudly. 'I don't want that! Nothing like *that*. Any case, how could you? Not *you*.'

'Sit down, son,' said Harris, turning his head towards a steel chair by the bedside table. He spoke like a man who had learnt how to give orders some time in his life, and Clive did as he was told. 'Now, let's talk straight,' Harris went on. 'Thanks to you, as you say, I'm going to be as good as bedridden for a fair long time, could be for ever. But whatever happens I don't propose to let it make any more difference to me than I can help. As far as it lies in my power, I'll see to it that I remain the same sort of chap I always have been.'

'Yeah.' Clive was all at sea again. 'You do that. Good for you.'

'I'm not going to let this thing change my character, whatever else it may or may not do. It's not going to turn me, you know, bitter.' A part of Harris's arm or hand moved a fraction, Clive thought. 'I just won't let it.'

'Right.'

'And that brings us to you,' said Harris.

'To *me*,' Clive realized out of the blue that he was afraid that this fellow was shaping up to forgiving him. 'What's all that got to do with me?'

'It was you made the accident happen. You said so yourself. No getting away from that.' Harris spoke as though he at least had got everything cut and dried. 'Now there's always someone that makes accidents happen. Street accidents, it'll be a car or other vehicle, and somebody's got to be driving it. Aeroplane accidents, somebody's forgotten to take the necessary –'

Clive interrupted him. 'But that's different! Don't you see?'

'All right then,' said Harris, not at all put out, 'let's take the car again. Suppose the driver's had a couple too many, and he knocks someone down. Now that's still –'

'Then he's a criminal! He's guilty!'

'I really don't know what you're getting so steamed up about, young fellow. Here I am telling you I don't feel bitter, I don't bear any malice, trying to put your mind at rest, and you start –'

Clive broke in for the third time, jumping up from where he had been sitting. A couple of things had become clear to him since he sat down. He was almost shouting when he said, 'I don't want my mind put at rest! That's what everyone else is on about! Trying to do their best for me and telling me I'm not to blame and didn't mean it and couldn't help it! But I thought at least you'd be different, you and your wife. I thought surely I could rely on you. You really had got something against me. That's what I thought until two minutes ago. What a mug, eh? You're as bad as all the others! You're bloody well forgiving me! You,' meaning Harris, 'after what I been and done to you! What more do you want? Like me to jump on you? Kick your head in? And you,' meaning Mrs Harris. 'It's your husband lying there. Why won't you tell me?' This time he meant both of them. 'Oh, God . . .'

Harris said sharply, 'Keep your voice down.'

'Sorry.' Clive swallowed and went on in a more normal voice, 'I just can't understand it. There you are, a cripple, or . . .' He went up to Mrs Harris. 'No – you were the one as wanted me put down hard, right? But then something happened. What was it?'

'Well, that solicitor, that Stone, he explained to us about the money.'

'Yeah, you said. Was that the only reason you changed your mind?'

'No,' said Mrs Harris. 'No, to be quite honest it

wasn't. I got to thinking, see? I'm not what you'd call religious, but I do know God doesn't want us to hate one another.' She actually gave a little smile. 'He wants us to forgive people their sins against us. It's our sacred duty.'

That set Clive going on another outburst. 'That's right! And to get our souls filled with love and light and peace! God wants us all to have a great time all the time never mind what we done! Say you're sorry and it hasn't bloody happened!' He quietened for a moment. 'Yeah. The old message. I might have known.'

Harris was looking completely baffled, almost worried. His head turned on the pillow. 'What are you *after*, lad?' he asked. 'What are you looking for?'

Then Clive really did shout. 'I'm looking for somebody who agrees with me about what I done!' And he turned his face away.

Mrs Harris stood up quickly and Harris said, 'You can't go making that sort of row and upset in here, my lad. You'd better get out right away.'

So Clive got out, past nurses, patients in dressing-gowns, visitors and other people coming to see what was going on.

8

About eleven o'clock that night Clive was sitting in the kitchen at home, at no. 9. There was nowhere else for him to be and nowhere else he could go to or face going to. He had looked in at the Lord Harry and come straight out again. The thought of food, any food, turned him up. Some of the time he had walked the streets, but at once forgot where he had been. There was no reply from Terry's number and he felt almost glad, anyway not sorry a bit. When he rang Paula her mother answered, and Paula was out, and the only real point about that was that he had no way of getting hold of one of the downer pills he had heard her say she used at night when she felt tensed up. He sat in front of the television in the kitchen and had the golf on.

Eventually he heard Don's key in the front door and realized he had been listening for it. After a minute, Don MacIntyre came out into the kitchen, and he was obviously not surprised either, seeing Clive there. Don had had a few beers, but he was nowhere near really drunk, which would have been a pity in the ordinary way because when he was absolutely gone he was a terrific guy, laughing, telling stories, always bringing something home for the family even if it was only a packet of crisps. The few beers tonight had gone nowhere near bringing on that change in him.

'Your mother gone to bed?' he asked.

Clive nodded his head without looking round.

'You watching this? You reading that paper?'

When Clive shook his head to both, Don switched off the golf, then turned round and stuck his hands on his hips. 'Well, what have you been doing with yourself all day then? Hanging about and lying on your bed if yesterday and the day before's anything to go by.'

'I done a fair crack of that, yeah,' said Clive. Then he went on like something out of the paper, 'But I also paid a visit to the hospital, where I had a conversation with Mr Harris, who is suffering from a severe back injury.'

'A joke, was it, seeing him, is that what you're saying?'

'Yeah, sort of, in a manner of speaking.'

'What's the matter with you, Clive? How was he, can you tell me that much? Is he ever going to walk again?'

'Nobody seems to know, Don.'

'I see. You and I got to have a talk, son.'

'I don't mind.'

Don brought out a tin of beer from the underneath part of the kitchen cupboard – he always said the fridge took all the flavour out of it – and poured it into a clean glass off the shelf. 'Now let's approach this quite calm-like,' he said, sitting down at the table.

'Fine with me,' said Clive.

Don looked at him again as though he was puzzled about something, but said, 'Right. We're going to face facts, you and me. You're a bloody young fool as broke into private property for no reason under the sun bar being idle and foolish – you must know I don't buy one ha'porth of that rubbish about you paying your mum back that cash you stole off her. As a consequence of which there's an ordinary decent bloke who's obviously not going to be getting around much in future. Do you follow me, Clive?'

'Yes. I follow you, Don.'

'Eh? Well . . . That court hearing today, so-called. You got off, didn't you? Got clear away with it. Probation. Means exactly nothing at all. I didn't care for that, you know. I felt it wasn't right. Not justice as I'd been brought up to understand it. A crime's a crime – you heard me say that. People ought to pay the proper penalty for what they done. Like I did that time. You understand.'

Clive said nothing to that, but he nodded his head a lot.

'Anyway, that's what I thought up to this morning,' said Don, and said nothing more for a moment or two. Then he went on, 'Well, after a bit we got to talking, your mother and me and that Miss Adams, and she said – it just never struck me before, but she ought to know, didn't she? Any road, the way it landed up, it come down to me wanting you to be punished for what you done the same as what I was for what I done. And that's no good – Miss Adams got me to see that. It was sort of like me wanting revenge.'

Just about then, Clive finally lost all hope. He would have trusted his stepfather, more than anybody else in the world, not to be shifted, not to come round, to stay where he had always been. And now here he was, that tough, plain Scotch bloke from up north with his vicars for grandfathers and his Bible ready to reach for and his stuff about responsibility, suddenly going on about not letting his personal feelings run away with him and looking at the situation objectively like all the others. He ended up by saying he understood now that the whole thing was a much broader problem than he had had any idea of.

'Yeah, isn't it just?' said Clive. 'It's a tremendously broad problem. It's such a broad problem everyone's in it. Society's to blame.'

'I wouldn't swear she didn't say something along those lines, ay,' said Don, trying a laugh. 'She does talk a fair bit, does Miss Adams.'

'Yeah, I got it. Society broke into Butterfields', and society run away from a watchman, and society fixed it up so he fell and broke his back. Yeah, that makes sense, don't it, Don? Stands to reason, you might say.'

'Eh? What I mean is, Clive, we've had our bust-ups

in the past, you and me, and I been hard on you now and then, I admit that, but, well . . .'

'What happened to the principle of the thing?'

'What was that? I don't remember.'

'When I took Mum's cash, and she said it was only a lousy tenner, and you said the amount didn't matter, it was the principle of the thing. Remember now?'

Don said in a straightforward way, 'Pay her back as soon as you can and we'll say no more about it. Anyhow, as I was telling you, after what's happened, what with today and all, I don't want you to feel that I'm the one that's letting you down.' And he pushed his chair back from the table and got up and stuck out his hand for Clive to shake.

Clive was touched by that. 'No, I'm sure you don't, Don,' he said, and got up too, and put his own hand affectionately on Don's shoulder for a moment, the first time he had ever touched his stepfather for any reason. But he held back from the handshake he was offered.

Somehow or other Clive got off to sleep quite quickly that night, and dreamt nothing that left much behind when he woke up. But when he did wake up he knew straight away it was for good – no sliding back and dozing around till he heard his mother going downstairs.

By his digital watch, one of a dozen Terry had been letting go at fifty p, it was 3:58. He tried to use up time getting out of bed, putting some clothes on, making tea, drinking it at the kitchen table over yesterday's paper. When he tried the radio he got only mush, and the TV film about some foreign place was hopeless, stupid. He could hear the traffic on the approach road and the flyover already thickening up, never mind it was still dark. Some fresh air might clear his head, he thought, even though his head felt quite clear, clear as if it had been swept through and left empty.

Outside, of course, it was quite a long way from dark, what with headlights and street lights and the reddish look over the top of the flyover that came from millions of lights further off. Clive started walking. After a bit he stopped at an all-night place, or one that had just opened, and after seeing he had the cash on him he went in for a cup of tea and a biscuit. By the time he had got the biscuit out of its wrapper it was mostly crumbs, and what he managed to get into his mouth tasted sweet and nothing else. The tea was all right, but he got bored with it half way. The place was less than half full and there was nobody there worth looking twice at. The strip lighting gave him an ache across his eyebrows which stopped when he went out and rested his forehead against the glass.

After some more walking, Clive saw that he was quite near the church where he had come to find the vicar, and he realized he had been sort of making for it for some time, perhaps all the way from home. St Christopher's. That was it. He found the door he had gone in by was locked or bolted, and went round the side, through scrubby grass and torn food-packets and falling-over, half-buried gravestones, and came to a smaller door, but that was fastened too. Next to it was a window, also small, and plain, not stained glass or anything. Clive bashed it in with a stone and was soon inside.

It was pretty dark there, of course, but he could make out the windows easily, there was a light on somewhere round a corner, and almost straight off he recognized where he was standing, near the corner where he had noticed the old girl kneeling and crying. So? Clive was looking helplessly around, not knowing what it was he was looking for, when after about a minute all the main lights came on at once and just for a moment it was like stepping out into the sunlight.

For a moment Clive was terrified, but then he saw the vicar, Robin Foster, crossing the church towards him.

'Clive! I'm sorry if I startled you. I heard a noise . . .'

'Oh, don't apologize, vicar. I mean, this is your place. Begin your day early, don't you?'

'I had to get some literature off to the newsagents to deliver with the papers.'

'Sorry, literature?'

'Hand-outs, pamphlets. About God's message.'

'Oh, in with the paper like gift offers. But sent from in here?'

'This is my administrative headquarters as well as my church and the rest of it.'

Foster had come up now and Clive took in his neat hairdo, half-quiff on forehead, and spotless pink-and-yellow shirt. 'I'm afraid what you heard was me breaking in. Window by the side door there. I –'

'Forget it.'

'Yeah. Well, I couldn't find a door that would open.'

'We have to keep the place locked up or vandals get in,' said Foster.

'Oh, some people think it's worth busting up, do they?'

'What are you doing here, Clive?'

'Don't you know? I thought you had an answer to everything. A, what is it, a pigeon-hole to stick everyone in. Like Miss Adams.' Clive was going to mention Sergeant Parnell, but left it. 'Well, what am I doing here, I sort of felt I had to go somewhere, and the only place I could think of was here. But I didn't know what for. But I thought, well, I'll go there, and maybe I'll find out what for.' He had another look round the building in the better light. 'But I haven't. It's like I've forgotten, only there's nothing to remember. Yeah. You went down and saw Harris and his wife the other day. Why d'you do that?'

'It was my Christian duty,' said Foster. 'I guessed – correctly, it seems – that you'd go to see them yourself, and I wanted to make sure, as far as it lay in my power, that they saw the situation in the right light. The light of mercy.'

'So that they let me off. Don't you ever wonder, vicar, if a bloke needs something . . . different to that, know what I mean?'

'You're troubled, Clive. I wish you'd tell me about it.'

'I tried you once before, mate, remember? And you went on about, er, God's forgiveness, wasn't it? Yeah.'

'God's forgiveness is there for anyone who stretches out his hand for it.'

Clive said, 'Sounds the easiest thing in the world, don't it? Cheers, Robin.'

When Clive had come out of the church, he turned in the direction away from home, though he had no idea where to go now. Soon the pavement narrowed where it went past a high wall, not the wall of anything in particular, just a wall. Clive turned his face to it, spreading his arms out sideways and pressing the palms of his hands against it.

Traffic was going by, but after a minute or so he was pretty sure he heard a car pull up somewhere behind him, and he certainly heard a man's voice call out,

'You over there. Is there anything wrong?'

At that, Clive swung round pretty sharp. As he had imagined in that fraction of a second, there was a police car just there at the kerb, and a man in plain clothes was getting out of it and coming towards him. But it was a stocky red-haired man he had never seen before, about thirty-five, anxious-looking, peering at him, asking him again if anything was wrong.

'No. No, I'm fine. Thank you very much.'

'Are you sure, sonny? You don't look well. Not sick, are you?'

'No, I'm okay. Really.'

'Oh. Good. Want a lift? Drop you anywhere?' The red-headed man was frowning, worried that things might not be all right. He was giving Clive what seemed to him the first straight look he had had for weeks.

'I'm fine, honest,' said Clive.

'If you're quite sure, now.'

'Yeah. Thanks.'

Reluctantly, the policeman went back to his car and in a moment was on his way. Clive started walking again, towards home this time, because that was what he might as well have done as not. The sun was up by now and it was going to be a beautiful day.